KEEPERS OF THE FIRE

KEEPERS OF THE FIRE

JOURNEY TO THE TREE OF LIFE BASED —ON— BLACK ELK'S VISION

story & paintings

by Eagle Walking Turtle

design
with illustrations adapted from the paintings
by Angela C. Werneke

BEAR & COMPANY, SANTA FE, NEW MEXICO

Bear & Company
P.O. Drawer 2860
Santa Fe, NM 87504

Cover & interior design, black & white illustrations:
Angela C. Werneke
Typography: Casa Sin Nombre, Ltd., Santa Fe
Printed in the United States of America

Second Printing

This book is for
Black Elk and Jesse McClain (Bluebird)

LIST OF PAINTINGS

ACKNOWLEDGEMENTS

The author, Eagle Walking Turtle, wishes to thank Black Elk for telling his beautiful visions to John Neihardt, so the people of our Mother Earth may feel the beauty of nature. Personal thanks go with love to my father and mother for instilling in my personality the recognition of the wisdom of nature; to Martin Red Bear, for believing in the spirit journey; to Jim Wood for his forceful encouragement; to Kaare Evensen for his spiritual love; to Jessa for teaching me patience; to my son Jesse for teaching me the meaning of the vision; to my wife Ruby for doing necessities while I did this; to our friend Rhonda Vlasik for her foresight and assistance with the text; to Gerry Hausman and Gerry Clow for believing in the vision; to Angela Werneke for designing the book; to Chuck Dailey and Carl Ponca at the Institute of American Indian Arts for displaying the paintings; and to the people at El Parian de Santa Fe Gallery.

THE TWO ROADS OF EAGLE WALKING TURTLE

by Gerald Hausman

When I first met Gary McClain—Eagle Walking Turtle—he had just completed the video of KEEPERS OF THE FIRE, and he was keeping his vision alive and burning by constantly playing the video in the shade-drawn darkened livingroom of his Pojoaque trailer. I would go see him and he would ask me in, and we would drink coffee and listen to the drums on the video and the chanting that reverberated the metal walls of his thinly disguised man-made tent. That the place was temporary could not have been more fitting, nor more sad. Because it was easy to visualize Gary and his Arapaho wife, Ruby, and the other assorted Sioux visitors singing and chanting in the high open meadow of a Teton summer.

There was a restlessness in Gary that made it difficult for him to remain seated for very long. It was late spring that year I met him and the cottonwood catkin-fluff was deep and downy in the courtyard of the trailers. I listened to the words of the drums while I viewed the countless images Gary had painted. What I saw was a visionary quest not unlike Black Elk's, in fact one stemming from the legendary Sioux's attempt to balance the forces of nature and people. Gary told me he had been hurt when young by bucking horses and later on by a lifetime commitment to art. The hurt was in his eyes along with the natural Choctaw sadness that was his heritage by birth. Yet there was also an Irish wisdom and laughing acceptance in his mouth that frequently turned subjects of sorrow into humor.

The paintings which were to become the pictures in this book showed the hard pilgrimage of truth that Gary himself had borne, but more importantly they showed the strides all Indians take in a world that must be met with faith in the unity of opposites. The personal travail of Gary's work was evident in every image his hand had touched, yet I saw the dream of his deliverance, his people's arrival upon the final threshold of Black Elk's vision—harmony.

For Gary, however, the world would fail to realize this message unless he—personally—as if entrusted by a spirit, might bear living witness to all that he had seen and felt in his mind's eye. It was not enough for him that he had delicately executed such fine paintings. And so, in a way, Gary was not letting go of his own message of delivery. He was holding onto a wild pony, clutching the mane with all ten of his tenacious fingers. Such is the life of many artists and Gary could not exempt himself from this consummate struggle. To be free—to set the world free—he must release that which was a part of him. That which he had entwined with his very soul.

One day when I drove over to Pojoaque to visit him, Gary and his family were gone. I learned from his friends that they'd headed back to

Arapaho country. I remembered the snowy blow of cottonwood down, how it swam visually before the oncoming tires of my car, in little rivers off the side of the road. I sat and meditated in the vacant hollow place where Gary McClain's temporary house had been, and I remembered Black Elk weeping upon the ridge of what he considered to be his life's failure.

I wondered if Gary felt that way, now, on the road somewhere, migrating into the many visions of paint and pain, darkness and light, hunger and wisdom, the end of the road where all things are swept together into magnificent oneness—under the Tree of Life, the joining of the Roads of Red and Black, triumph and travail. And I got my answer there in the bright sad sunlight of early fall—Gary and his paintings would live together in a book which someone, somewhere, would publish. I knew it then as I know it now: it would be. As certain as Black Elk brought rain that day he wept for the sorrow of his nation, and for all Indian people everywhere who have walked the Good Red Road of peace, the hard Black Road of difficulty.

The book you hold in your hands is the joining of the roads. Peace lies within these pages.

EDITOR'S NOTE

Black Elk, an Oglala Sioux visionary, was an old man when John G. Neihardt, the interviewer of *Black Elk Speaks*, first met him. It was May in the year 1931 when poet Neihardt visited Black Elk's home at the Pine Ridge Agency near Manderson, South Dakota. Nearly blind and speaking no English, Black Elk agreed to "tell his story" to Neihardt so the world would know his "Great Vision for men."

He was born in December—the Moon of the Popping Trees—in 1863 and his great vision came to him nine years later. In the vision he saw that where the "good road and the road of difficulties" intersected there was a holy place wherein a sacred tree was growing. The good red road and the shielding tree of Black Elk's vision represented, for him and for all "two-leggeds, four-leggeds, the wings of the air and all green things that live," a world of divine love.

Historically, Black Elk's supreme vision could not have come at a better or worse time in Native American life. It was the end of the old ways, the splintery beginning of the modern and empty new. The faith in healing and the great commitment of his vision separated Black Elk from the merely warrior members of his tribe. What he saw enabled him to fight against the whites, the Wasichus, with more than deadly aim of arrow or gun. He fought with faith. Thus the messianic message travels down the convoluted airways of lost time and speaks to us today as it did when he first told his story to Neihardt in 1931.

Eagle Walking Turtle's vision is inspired by Black Elk's and owes its vital force to it. Both men could not rest until other eyes had seen what was said from within and until the good red road was in balance with all that haunts the troubled soul of humankind.

G.A.H., Tesuque, NM 1986

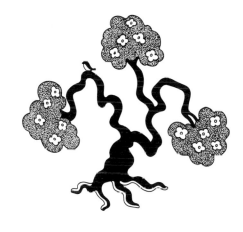

PREFACE

Black Elk was a great warrior and a great man of visions. His greatest vision was of all people walking in balance with spiritual and physical life and with all life on our Mother Earth. He said we must water the roots of the tree that grows at the place where these roads cross and she will grow, flower, and fill with singing birds. What he meant by these words is that if we treat each other with respect and treat our Mother Earth and her life with respect, we will all be able to live here together in peace and harmony and we will all be happy and receive everything we need from our Earth Mother.

And, we must also give thanks and respect to the one that created us all and created our Earth Mother, the Great Mystery, for without this powerful force and this great gift of creation we would not exist, nor would our Mother Earth.

The story, KEEPERS OF THE FIRE, is based upon a real legend found in many tribes, about an old man who appeared to many cultures with a message. It is a spiritual journey, without basis in historical fact or time sequence, written and painted by the author in response to this legend left by Black Elk and others like him.

KEEPERS OF THE FIRE

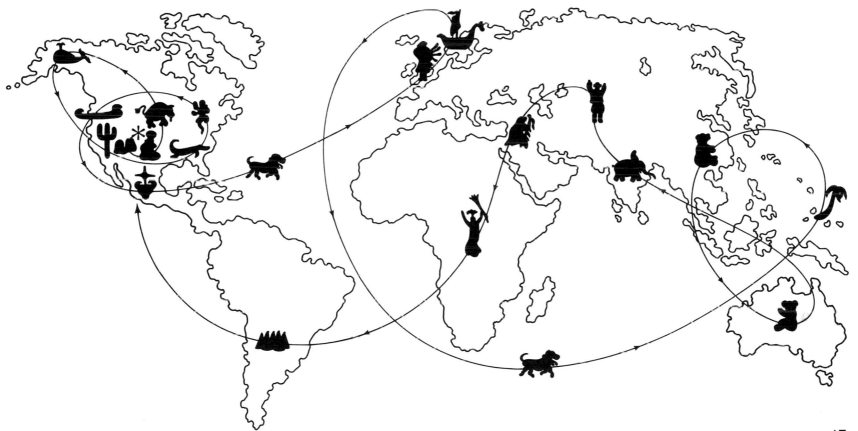

MY NAME IS BLACK ELK. I AM Lakota and I am an old man now. But I can still see the Spirit of my people standing tall—above snows and grasses that have been—when buffalo herds were wide as day and the earth stayed young.

LONG AGO, AS A YOUNG WARRIOR, I was lying ill in my mother's lodge when the Great Mystery talked to me, my Grandchildren. The Great Mystery gave me a vision of beauty, and I recovered from my illness so I might tell the people and creatures of our Mother Earth. Blue Spotted Horse, our great Medicine Man, said my vision was for all creatures: the two-leggeds, the four-leggeds, the ones that fly, the ones that swim in the waters, and the ones that slither in the grasses.

BLUE SPOTTED HORSE SAID that we all walk two roads in our life. One is the Red Road of spirit that begins in the place where the sun lives. It runs across the world to the place where the Great White Giant lives. The other road is the Black Road of life, the hard road of difficulty, that begins in the place where the sun rises and all the days of people begin, and runs across the world to the place where the Black Thunder Beings live and all the days of people end. Blue Spotted Horse said that the Tree of Life grows in the place where the roads cross. That is the Tree we must find and water, so it will bloom and fill with singing birds.

I ASKED BLUE SPOTTED HORSE IF HE would travel to take my vision to all people and creatures of our Mother Earth. I asked him to see if the Tree of Life still lives. So, he put on his best red blanket with the black crosses. And, he took up his red-and-white staff. He raised his arms in praise and said he would take my vision to the people and creatures of our Mother Earth and find out if the root of the Tree was still alive.

21

A ND SO, WE BUILT A COUNCIL
fire to honor my vision. As the
sun set behind the mountains, we
smoked together the sacred pipe and we promised

to meet by this sacred fire again. Three brother friends—Charging Cat, High Horse, and Blue Mouse —trapped four of the tiny wild horses that live in holes by the river to pull Blue Spotted Horse's travois and to haul his parfleches full of food. With great ceremony, they presented their gift to Blue Spotted Horse.

EARLY THE NEXT SUNRISE, Blue Spotted Horse and his dog Saggie began their long journey.

I N THE MOON OF CRACKING TREES, Blue Spotted Horse and his companion found people who lived in a great cave inside a mountain. These people hunted deer and other small creatures and always thanked the spirits of the animals who gave their lives so that the people might eat.

They gathered berries and always thanked our Mother Earth for her gifts that grew so that the people might live. Blue Spotted Horse told them of my vision—that people walk in balance with all life on our Mother Earth. Though they already knew about the vision, none among them knew where the Tree of Life could be found.

So, THEY LISTENED AND welcomed the words of Blue Spotted Horse as he talked about the Great Mystery, the great gift of creation. As he spoke his last words, happy cries of blessing and thanks filled the air. Some of the people built fires and others began roasting meat and preparing the feast. When the night grew cold, Blue Spotted Horse and Saggie went with the people into their home in the mountain.

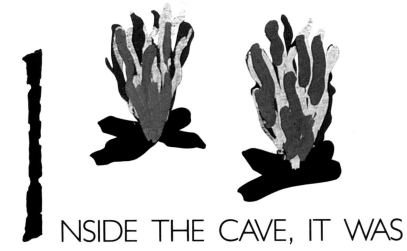

NSIDE THE CAVE, IT WAS warm and the travellers were made welcome. The cave people built council fires and many voices of song echoed from the walls in honor of my vision.

AFTER RESTING AND FEASTING and enjoying the sweet spring water, Blue Spotted Horse, Saggie, and three new travellers—Chief Ewat, Nahathosa, and Bluebird—prepared to continue their journey. As they left, there was a great shout of farewell. The trilling of the women carried the travellers' hearts high as they found their path.

I N THE MOON OF LEAVES BREAKING
Forth, as the sun fell beyond our mountains, the
travellers found people who live in mud dwellings.
The pueblo people welcomed them with a feast of
blue corn and many-colored gourds of squash.

THE PEOPLE CAME DOWN THE LONG ladders that led from the top of the great mud dwelling to the ground and, dressed in brightly colored cloth, they danced and sang to honor the news of my vision. They built four council fires that burned long into the night. The celebration with dancing and feasting continued for four days and the people were happy.

THEY ASKED THE TRAVELLERS TO STAY, but Blue Spotted Horse told them they must go on to search for others to tell of my vision and to search for the Tree of Life. So, with their parfleches full of oven bread, they left the next sunrise.

34

IN THE MOON OF DRY GRASSES,
the travellers found people who live in lodges made
of animal skins, as we do. The plains people welcomed Blue Spotted Horse with dried bison meat
and chokecherry gravy, which they had prepared for
the cold days to come.

AS MY FRIEND BEGAN TELLING the tipi dwellers about my vision and how we must water the roots of the Tree that grows at the place where the roads cross, they built four council fires and people sat and listened, nodding as the medicine man spoke.

WHEN THE SUN ROSE THE NEXT morning, the sacred red pipe was smoked and raised to the sun in celebration and thanks to the Great Mystery. Many honor songs were sung that day, and the drums and songs were heard far into the night, as the ceremony honored my vision that is for all people.

THE NEXT SUNRISE, THE PEOPLE filled the parfleches with much dried meat and dried berries and Blue Spotted Horse, Nahathosa, Bluebird, Chief Ewat, and Saggie started their long journey to that place where the Great White Giant lives.

ɔɔɔɔɔI T WAS A LONG JOURNEY
and after many moons had passed the travellers
came to a place where the people live in ice dwellings. They wear thick furs for protection from the
cold and they say the sun is not often warm.

HE PEOPLE WELCOMED THE travellers with a feast of dried fish and caribou gravy and when they learned of my vision, four council fires were started in pots that burn whale oil. Blue Spotted Horse told them of how my vision honored them and how my vision honored their sacred white herbs and their sacred white goose feather.

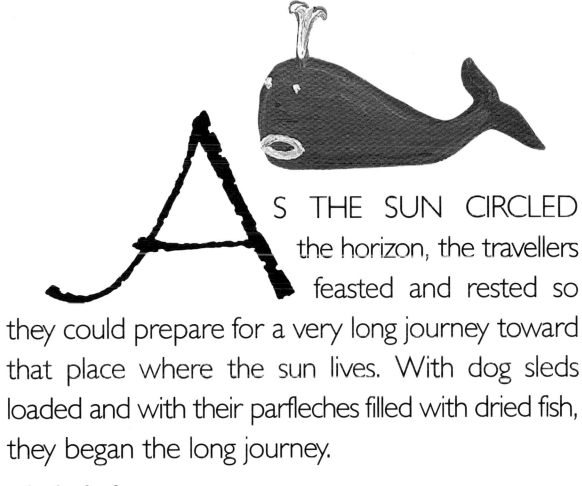

As THE SUN CIRCLED the horizon, the travellers feasted and rested so they could prepare for a very long journey toward that place where the sun lives. With dog sleds loaded and with their parfleches filled with dried fish, they began the long journey.

THEY FIRST MET A YOUNG BOY WHO told them how the people in this harsh land had always travelled from place to place in order to find enough food to eat. Then the boy took them to the home of his people where they saw green stalks growing, where only white sand and rock had been before. As Blue Spotted Horse marvelled at this, the chief of the desert people appeared, followed by more of the villagers, who carried great pots of rabbit stew and corn meal.

FOUR COUNCIL FIRES WERE BUILT AND AS the people feasted, Blue Spotted Horse told them of my vision. He told how I had seen the place where the sun lives and how six sacred branches and hoops of the people intertwine with one great hoop. The people were filled with great joy and gave thanks to the Great Mystery in a celebration of singing and dancing. At the next sun, as Blue Spotted Horse left the wickiup of the chief to continue the search, the songs of the desert people filled the air and went with the travellers as they travelled on.

KEEPERS OF THE FIRE
© EAGLE X WALKING TU

N THE MOON OF NEW GRASSES, Blue Spotted Horse, Nahathosa, Blue-bird, Chief Ewat, and Saggie travelled toward the home of the great waters, where the water is warm and salty. On the way, they found people who live in the wet and swampy places beyond our plains. The swamp people live in shelters made of grasses or in log houses dug into the river bank of the running waters that flowed to the great waves. The villagers welcomed the travellers with a feast of boiled alligator and many kinds of fish.

WEARY FROM THE LONG journey, Blue Spotted Horse dreamed deeply that night, as the river water softly lapped against the shore of the village. The next morning, as the sun rose through the mist, Blue Spotted Horse told the swamp people about my vision and the Tree of Life. He told them that all life is sacred and that all living things are the children of one mother and their father is one Spirit.

A S BLUE SPOTTED HORSE TALKED, a few of the people sat with long sticks and drew pictures and word symbols into the soft ground surrounding the medicine man. At his last words, our Mother Earth lay covered with signs and symbols telling the story of my vision, and the swamp people rejoiced with a celebration to honor the Great Mystery.

52

EVEN AS THE PEOPLE GAVE THANKS, BLUE Spotted Horse prepared for a longer journey— toward that place where the Great White Giant lives. The travellers were given new parfleches made of alligator hides, which the villagers had filled with much dried fish. After another peaceful night of rest, as the red sun rose and lit the path, Blue Spotted Horse, Chief Ewat, Nahathosa, Bluebird, and Saggie travelled on.

IN THE MOON WHEN THE BERRIES Blacken, the travellers arrived in a place where the people live in longhouses and there are many trees. It was the Moon When the Air Is Smoky and the sacred colors were beautiful in the trees and in the land. The forest people welcomed the travellers with a great feast of wild turkey, as Blue Spotted Horse told them of my vision. The forest people nodded and smiled as

54

Blue Spotted Horse spoke and as he finished, one among them stood to say that they, too, knew of the vision. This one then spoke of Deganawida, a great prophet whose vision of four snakes in four colors was the same in spirit as my vision-gift.

FOUR SACRED FIRES WERE BUILT IN THE four directions to honor the Great Mystery and my vision that is for all people. There was a radiant joy among them. They urged the travellers to stay and build houses and join their community, but Blue Spotted Horse told them they must go on to tell others of my vision and to search for the Tree of Life.

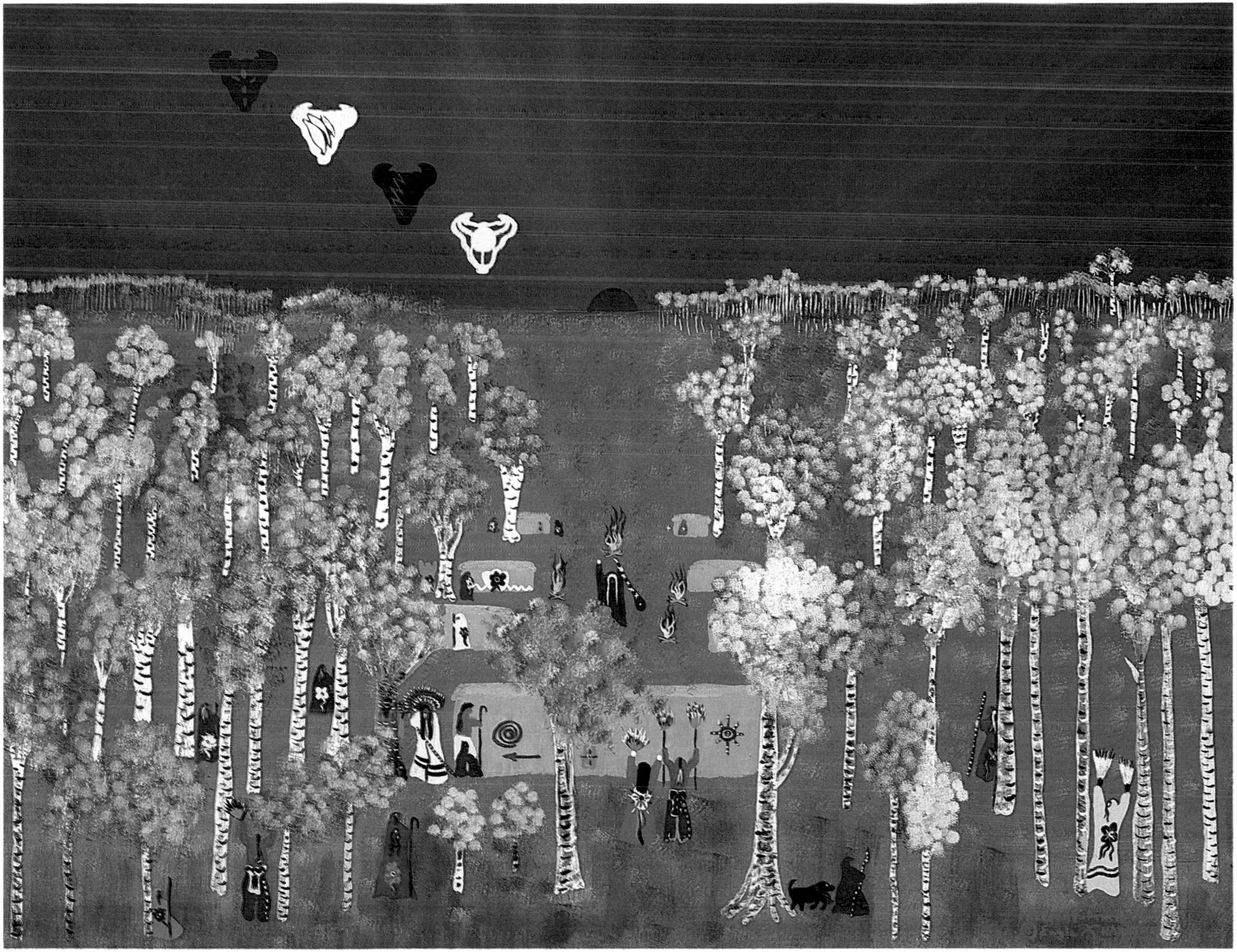

SO, AFTER SEVERAL SUNRISES, the travellers prepared to go on with parfleches filled with dried deer meat and dried berries. They arose with a new sunrise and continued on toward that place where the sun goes away and there is a great water that is cold and tastes salty.

AFTER MANY SUNRISES, the travellers came to the place of the great waves where the water is cold and salty. There they saw a wonderful thing—trees, very tall trees with carved faces of birds and animals. The people of this sea-shore place called the carved trees totems and made Blue Spotted Horse, Chief Ewat, Nahathosa, Bluebird, and Saggie very welcome in their village.

THE COASTAL PEOPLE SET OUT A great feast of fish and sea creatures who live in shells and many baskets of berries and strange foods brought from the cold, salty water. As they feasted, Blue Spotted Horse told the people about my vision, and as he spoke, they raised their hands and hearts to honor the Great One that is the creator of all men and women and the creator of all creatures.

H E TOLD THE PEOPLE OF THE great wave water how the vision teaches us two-leggeds to share in life with all our brothers and sisters, and with the four-leggeds and the wings of the air and with the sea creatures and all living things. When he finished speak-

62

ing, the people gave thanks to the Great Mystery for the Tree of Life, and Blue Spotted Horse gave thanks for the safe journey and for being among the good people.

IN THE MOON WHEN THE CORN IS Taken In, they encountered a huge tribe that live in stone houses. There the people had built majestic stone temples with many steps from the ground to the very top. The tribe welcomed them with many cries and shouts of greeting and took the travellers to meet their great chief, Quetzalcoatl, the plumed and feathered serpent.

A S BLUE SPOTTED HORSE told him about my vision, the morning star rose and Quetzalcoatl knew these words were for all people and that it was a vision of peace and harmony. It was good, it was very, very good. As the new sun rose, the great chief told his people the words of Blue Spotted Horse and a huge roar sounded through the valley in praise of the Great Mystery. A grand feast was prepared in honor of my vision and the celebration lasted for many more sunrises.

WHEN THEY LEARNED OF THE travellers' next destination, the people built great boats of reeds which they supplied with parfleches full of dried meats and fruits. With hearts full of happiness, Blue Spotted Horse, Chief Ewat, Nahathosa, Bluebird, and Saggie slept many hours before the new sun rose. Two of the tribe, High Bear and Everlasting Life, joined the travellers that day on their journey to find the Tree of Life. As they left, the people were still praising my vision.

AFTER LEAVING THE LAND OF
the people of the stone temples in
the place where the sun lives, Blue
Spotted Horse and his companions continued their
sacred journey in the boats made of reeds. They
sailed for many moons across the great salty water
toward that place where the sun
rises and where all the days of people begin. It was the Moon When the New Flowers
Bloom; the land was green and the air smelled

good. Once on shore, the travellers met people without much color in their skin. This pale tribe welcomed Blue Spotted Horse and his companions with feasting and dancing and strange music that hurt their ears.

THE MEDICINE MAN FIRST TOLD THE people that in my vision I saw the color red and the sacred red pipe in the direction where the sun rises and the morning star lives. He said that in my vision, I saw the color white in the direction where the Great White Giant lives and how the sacred white goose and the sacred white herb stand for the cleansing and healing that is brought by the winds of winter.

BLUE SPOTTED HORSE TOLD them that in my vision I saw the color black in the direction where the Black Thunder Beings live and the sun goes away each day and all the days of people end. He told them about the wooden cup, which pours the rain to sustain growth, and the power of the bow to kill for food so we may live.

B LUE SPOTTED HORSE TOLD
them about the six sacred branches, which stand for growth, and the
sacred hoops of the people, which stand for unity,
in that direction where the sun lives. There was
more music and dancing and the people raised their
arms to honor my vision from the Great Spirit.

THE PEOPLE URGED THE TRAVELLERS to stay, but when Blue Spotted Horse said they were on a long journey to find the Tree of Life, the people filled the travellers' parfleches with a strange, round root-food. When a new sun rose, they danced and played music as the travellers continued on their sacred journey.

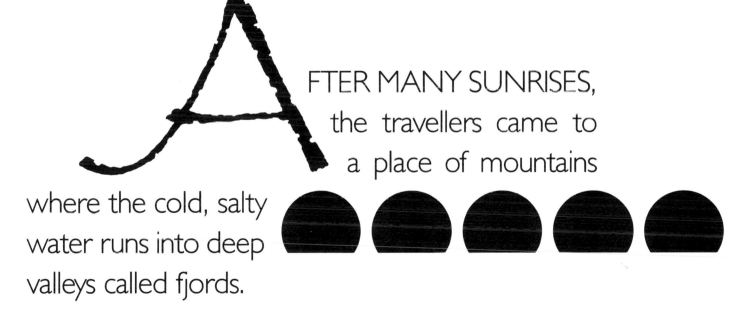

AFTER MANY SUNRISES, the travellers came to a place of mountains where the cold, salty water runs into deep valleys called fjords.

HERE, THEY MET PEOPLE WHO wear horns on their heads, like our buffalo dancers, and travel the cold water-waves in boats with carved heads of animals on their fronts and huge squares of hides that catch the winds to move them through the waters. This was a tribe of great warriors who loved life and loved being brave, as we do. Their chief was called the Red One and he welcomed the strangers with

a grand feast of wild bird. When Blue Spotted
Horse told him of my vision, Chief Red One rejoiced
in the wisdom and peace and harmony; he honored
the healing and cleansing; he praised the powers of
the Great Mystery.

AS HE TOLD BLUE SPOTTED Horse he would carry my vision to the people of his land, there was a great sounding of horn trumpets to proclaim our visit. The horns echoed in the mountains and trees and over the waters.

ONE OF THIS TRIBE, RED Hawk, joined us in our sacred search that day and it was good, it was very, very good. When the travellers again prepared to journey on, the Red One gave them the gift of a ship which would speed them across the water to a place where it was warmer. As Blue Spotted Horse and his friends sailed away, they could hear the horn trumpets clearing the way for safety on their journey.

AFTER MANY MOONS, THE travellers found a warm and sunny land surrounded by warm salty waters. Here, the trees were tall and thin and without branches; round stones grew in the tops of these trees and were filled with a white liquid that is good to drink. People wearing clothes made of grasses and bright cloth met them on the shore, and they were welcomed with music and dancing and strings of fragrant and colorful flowers.

WHEN BLUE SPOTTED HORSE told the island people of my vision, they were filled with joy. He said we must give thanks to the Great Mystery, the one who created us all and created our Earth Mother, for without this powerful force and this great gift of creation, we would not exist nor would our Mother Earth. The people celebrated his words with a feast of many fruits and fishes and sweet drinks that made the travellers happy. Blue Spotted Horse and his companions rested for many sunrises and feasted with the island people, while Saggie splashed in the warm sea water and rolled in the white sand.

FINALLY CAME THE TIME FOR LEAVING; the travellers filled their parfleches with dried fruit as the villagers stacked many coconuts on board their ship. One of the village people, White Bear, joined the travellers that day. At the next sunrise, the island people pushed the big boat back onto the water-waves and the travellers continued their search for the Tree of Life.

AFTER MANY MOONS, the warm winds blew the travellers into a land where the people live in houses with peaked roofs. The windows and doors of these houses were made of paper. The people of this land were quite small with bright eyes that turned down in the corners. The people welcomed the travellers with much courtesy.

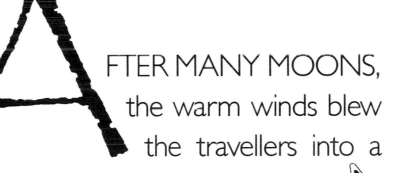

AS BLUE SPOTTED HORSE began telling their spiritual leader about my vision, the people listened with quiet politeness. He told them that my vision was for all people and all creatures. He said it was the wish of the Great Mystery that we all live in peace and harmony together on our Mother Earth and that we

must honor our Earth Mother and her life and keep
safe all her creatures. As the medicine man finished,
the people bowed deeply at the waist and put their
hands together with the fingers pointed to
the sky in silent praise of the Great One that
is the creator of all life.

SOME OF THEM BEGAN building four fires in four directions to celebrate my vision and as more and more people gathered, a hum of soft voices spread the word of the Tree of Life to the newcomers. They soon prepared a feast of raw fishes and bowls of white grain which they grew in shallow water holes on their land.

BLUE SPOTTED HORSE AND his companions feasted and rested for many suns and were very comfortable and happy with these people, but when the sunrise came, they climbed aboard their great boat and sailed away again toward another land to continue the search and spread the news of my vision.

IN THE MOON OF FALLING LEAVES,
the group sailed to a land where, at first,
they saw no people. They walked for many
sunrises over dry, parched ground and saw strange
and exotic creatures. Saggie made friends as they

searched for a village: first, with a small brown-and-white bearlike creature with a gentle face and black rings around his eyes. His next playmate was very unusual, indeed, as it stood upright like a two-legged one but carried its young in a pocket in its belly and jumped very high as it chased Saggie around the desert.

FINALLY, THEY CAME TO A VILLAGE AND the people marvelled at the strangers and welcomed them with a huge feast of platypus stew. These people were hunters and stalked their animal food with sticks curved in the shape of a new moon.

BLUE SPOTTED HORSE BEGAN to tell of my vision and the bush people understood and gave thanks to the Great Mystery, the creator of all creatures, and to our Earth Mother, from whom they received all things for living. They built four fires between their sacred stones and it was good, it was very, very good.

B

LUE SPOTTED HORSE AND HIS companions spent many sunrises in this strange land and saw many more new and wonderful things, but finally came the day for leaving. Two of the bush people, Minisa and Mano Luta, joined our group that day and after filling the parfleches with dried insects, the group journeyed on.

IN THE MOON OF CLOUDS MOVING Fast Across the Sky, Blue Spotted Horse and his companions came to a vast land of mountains, plains, and jungles. They were met by great multitudes of people who welcomed the group with a huge feast of yellow rice and foods made with a spice called curry.

AS BLUE SPOTTED HORSE BEGAN telling the people about my vision and the Tree of Life, more and more people began arriving to hear his words. Soon, there were so many listening that the land upon which they stood was no longer visible. The medicine man told them about the two roads, the

red and the black, and said we must water the roots of the Tree that grows at the place where these roads cross and it will grow and flower and fill with singing birds. In this land of so many different tribes, these words of peace and harmony were very important, indeed, and the people listened with great respect for the wisdom of the vision.

THE TRAVELLERS SPENT MANY sunrises going from village to village, meeting great numbers of people and spreading our message. One more traveller, Rhonda, joined the sacred pilgrimage on the last day and it was good, it was very, very good.

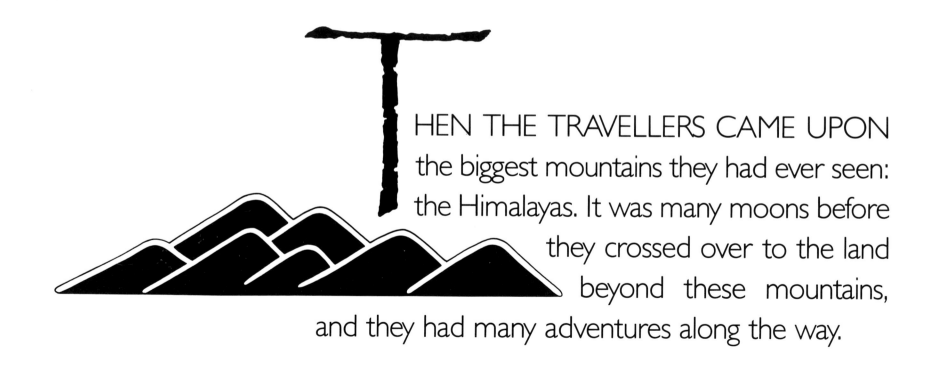

THEN THE TRAVELLERS CAME UPON the biggest mountains they had ever seen: the Himalayas. It was many moons before they crossed over to the land beyond these mountains, and they had many adventures along the way.

FINALLY, THEY ARRIVED AT A SNOW-covered place where the land stretched on and on as far as they could see in all directions. The medicine man and his companions were met by people who presented them with great coats of animal fur and then led them inside their warm dwellings. Roaring fires warmed the travellers as Blue Spotted Horse began telling them about my vision and the Tree of Life.

WHILE HE SPOKE, A FEAST OF sturgeon eggs and a strong drink made of goat's milk was made ready. As he spoke his final words, a huge celebration was held in a big open space made of stone, which was surrounded by buildings with rounded roofs shaped like our turnips. When Blue Spotted Horse told them they were on a journey to all people and all creatures, they filled their parfleches with bags of yogurt and sent along guides to lead them through the vast, snow-covered land. And so, they continued on their journey.

IN THE MOON OF LEAVES BREAK-
ing Forth, Blue Spotted Horse and his
companions arrived in a land where there
are spirits of holy men. Many people dressed
in light-colored, long, flowing robes met them
as they entered the first village; as protection
from the heat, these people wore light cloth
wrapped around their heads so that only their
eyes were visible.

B

LUE SPOTTED HORSE AND
the rest of the travellers sat
down on brightly colored blankets and the
medicine man began telling the people
about my vision of all people walking in
balance with spiritual and physical life
and with all life on our Mother Earth.

THEY LISTENED AS HE TOLD THEM that we must give thanks and respect to the Great Mystery, the one that created us all and created our Mother Earth. For without this powerful force and this great gift of creation, we would not exist nor would our Mother Earth. A great song of thanks was sung to the Great Mystery that day, and the villagers prepared a feast of flat bread and goat meat.

AT THE NEXT SUNRISE, AS THE travellers prepared to leave, the people of the village filled their parfleches with small black fruit of the vine which have a hard stone inside. Then, the chief of the village gave them the gift of large animals with great humps on their backs; these creatures needed very little water and were necessary for travelling across the vast desert which surrounded the village.

ONE MORE TRAVELLER, Morning Star, joined the sacred travellers that day and it was good, it was very, very good. As they were preparing to go on with the sacred journey, Blue Spotted Horse and his companions noticed that one of the trees had begun to bloom and fill with singing birds. The trees had all been barren upon their arrival.

AFTER LEAVING THE HOLY LAND, the sacred journey continued to a great continent where the travellers found many amazing and colorful creatures. They marvelled at white horses with black stripes and tall, long-necked, yellow-and-brown creatures which fed on leaves in the tree tops. As they found their path, they saw cats of all sizes and colors: shiny black ones with bright, green eyes; tawny-colored cats with much fur around their faces; and even small yellow cats with black spots. Birds and flowers of all colors filled the jungle.

Keepers of the Fire 20
©EAGLE × WALKING

BLUE SPOTTED HORSE AND his companions met very dark-skinned people who hunted with spears and lived in huts made of brown grasses. At sunset, a feast of roasted meat, sweets, and red fruit was prepared as the medicine man told them about my vision and the Tree of Life. Four fires were built in the four directions to honor our Earth Mother, the Great Mystery, and my vision that is for all creatures.

I T WAS IN THE MOON of East Winds when the group sailed away from the beautiful land filled with wonderful, colorful creatures.

WHEN THE MOON OF FALLING Leaves was full, the happy group sailed to a rocky shoreline and began a long journey on foot. They climbed for many sunrises into the mountains until the air grew very thin and the clouds surrounded them. When they reached the top, they found a village built of flat stones and mud, like villages they had visited earlier. Dark-skinned people greeted them with a feast of beans and a hot, black drink that smelled strong and good.

AFTER RESTING FROM THE long journey on the water-waves, Blue Spotted Horse told the native people about my vision; the mountain villagers built four fires

in the four directions and praised the Great One that created all creatures and all life.

THE NEXT SUNRISE, WHILE THE people of this village known as Machu Picchu still celebrated, the travellers began the journey inland down the mountain. After many sunrises and many villages, they reached the foot of the mountain. As the group walked toward that direction where the Great White Giant lives, they came to a wide river called the Amazon. They met herders, hunters, farmers, and food gatherers along the way.

THE LAND CHANGED WITH THE moons and the climate became warmer as they walked north. Always, they were given food and were invited to stay with the native peoples, but Blue Spotted Horse said they must continue the journey so that everyone would learn of the beauty of my vision that is for all creatures.

THEN, ONE SUNRISE, Blue Spotted Horse, Saggie, and their many companions, arrived at my lodge. . .

A

GAIN WE SMOKED THE SACRED red pipe by the sacred fire and we gave thanks to the Great Mystery for their safe journey. Blue Spotted Horse spoke for many hours. He talked of the many different peoples and lands he had visited and the wonderful creatures he had seen. And it was good, Grandchildren, it was very, very good.

AFTER A LONG SILENCE, Blue Spotted Horse spoke again. He said that his great journey to all people and creatures of our Earth Mother had shown him that the roots of the Tree of Life *are* still alive! They are alive in the hearts of each one of us, and if we water the Tree, it will grow and bloom and fill with singing birds.

123

BLUE SPOTTED HORSE THEN went on his last journey—to join the Great Mystery in the spirit world. The people of our Earth Mother joined together in a great celebration of feasting and dancing and singing to honor the medicine man and the Great Mystery and our Mother Earth.

MAY WE ALL CONTINUE TO water the roots of the Tree of Life so our Earth Mother will never die!

ABOUT THE AUTHOR

Eagle Walking Turtle is a Choctaw/Irish artist and writer who portrays the visions of Native Americans in his work. His paintings have been exhibited widely throughout the United States and he is currently showing at galleries in New Mexico and California. He studied at Kansas State University and the University of Wyoming. Eagle Walking Turtle lives with his wife Ruby and son Jesse in Arroyo Jacona, a small community north of Santa Fe, New Mexico.

ABOUT THE DESIGNER

Angela Werneke has been a graphic designer and illustrator for seventeen years. She received her B.F.A. in graphic design from Kent State University. Recent books Angela has illustrated include *The Book of Sufi Healing* (Inner Traditions International, 1985); *The Yoga of Herbs* (Lotus Press, 1986); *The Eye of the Centaur* (Llewelyn, 1986). She sees her work as a means of healing and nurturing the Earth and its inhabitants. She makes her home in Nambé, New Mexico.

OTHER BOOKS OF RELATED INTEREST
BY BEAR & COMPANY

ORIGINAL BLESSING
A Primer in Creation Spirituality
by Matthew Fox

MEDITATIONS WITH ANIMALS
A Native American Bestiary
by Gerald Hausman

MANIFESTO FOR A GLOBAL CIVILIZATION
by Matthew Fox & Brian Swimme

MEDITATIONS WITH THE HOPI
A Centering Book
by Robert Boissiere

THE UNIVERSE IS A GREEN DRAGON
A Cosmic Creation Story
by Brian Swimme

MEDITATIONS WITH NATIVE AMERICANS
Lakota Spirituality
by Paul Steinmetz

GREEN POLITICS
The Global Promise
by Fritjof Capra & Charlene Spretnak

MEDITATIONS WITH THE NAVAJO
Navajo Stories of the Earth
by Gerald Hausman

Contact your local bookseller or write:
BEAR & COMPANY
P.O. Drawer 2860
Santa Fe, NM 87504